Prince Valiant

FIGHTS ATTILA THE HUN

By HAROLD FOSTER

HAL FOSTER

HASTINGS HOUSE

Publishers   New York

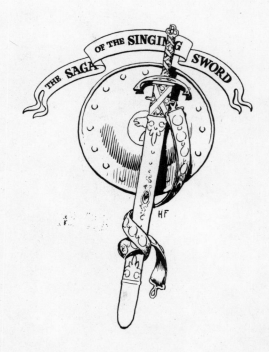

THE SAGA OF THE SINGING SWORD

Printed in U. S. A.

And so, as the old story tells, King Arthur, having driven the Saxon force out of Britain with grievous slaughter, gazed proudly at his knights and warriors assembled about him on the still smoking field of battle. His eyes fell upon the slender youth who, though not yet a knight, had performed such mighty deeds of valor that day as to leave no further doubt he had fairly earned the right to knighthood. The king spoke out: "Kneel, Prince Valiant!"

Prince Valiant, stained with the blood of enemies, weary of body but flushed with the joy of victory, dropped to his knees. Thus he remained with head bowed until he felt the touch of Arthur's sword Excalibur upon his shoulder and heard the king's "Arise, Prince Valiant, Knight of the Round Table!" Never had the youth heard words so sweet.

And now the great assemblage on the battlefield was hailing the new knight. Around him thronged Sir Launcelot, Sir Galahad, mighty Sir Tristram, Sir Gawain the Lighthearted, Sir Ector, Sir Kay the Seneschal and many another whose prowess was already legend. And all embraced Sir Valiant in honored fellowship. But in all that gallant host the most joyous was Val's father, the exiled King of Thule.

Then, turning to Val's father, King Arthur said: "And you, O rightful King of Thule, ask me what favor you will and it shall be granted for your son's sake."

Pointing to the water's edge where the sun was sinking blood-red behind the smoke of the burning enemy fleet, Val's father answered: "Save me but one

enemy ship from the flames that my tall son and I and the few brave warriors who fled with me to safety and freedom in Britain — and who still honor me with the name of king — may sail once more to our beloved homeland and wrest it from the bloody grip of Sligon the Tyrant!"

The request was at once granted. "Yet do I speak rashly," King Arthur said, frowning as he looked upon the burning ships; "for I see no sound and seaworthy vessel left!" But then, noticing a smile on Val's face, he added: "Unless, in truth, this new knight, your son, foresaw your return to Thule and wisely preserved one goodly vessel from the flames."

Then Val acknowledged freely that he had indeed saved one of the ships to speed his father's return to Thule. "God prosper your adventure," Arthur said, and with that he and his knights mounted and rode back to Camelot, leaving Val and his father and their stout-hearted little band of loyal warriors to prepare for the perilous journey to the north. So all set about making the ship ready. Then from the battlefield they gathered up arms, equipment and provisions and stowed them aboard. And after snatching a few hours' rest, they committed themselves to God's will, and fared forth under a favoring wind at the morning tide. And in a short time they gained the open sea and Britain faded slowly in the mist.

Yet Val, gazing back, sighed in seeing Britain fade. It was not that Britain meant peace and safety; and that ahead, in the unhappy land of Thule, death waited their coming. No, he had other reasons. For twelve years, since that fearful night when Sligon's treachery fell upon them like fire and drove

4

them to the sea, far-off Britain had been their refuge and their home. On an island in the depths of the mysterious fens in East Britain, his father the king, and his frail mother, and the handful of loyal warriors who had chosen exile to tyranny, had started life anew, strangers in a strange new land. Here, in Britain, Val had grown out of pampered boyhood into stalwart youth; a prince still — but a prince with no greater riches than the apparel on his back, the wit in his head, and the courage in his heart. Here, in Britain's soil, was his mother's grave. Here, under Britain's sky, he had first dreamed of knighthood. And here, under Britain's moon, he had stolen his first kiss from a fair maid.

Here, too, in Britain, he had met Sir Gawain the Lighthearted, whose quips were as sharp as his lance, and whose laughter was a shield no foe could pierce. Him Val had served as squire, and through days never to be forgotten had adventured and quested and fought and loved and made merry and, above all, had learned all that Gawain could teach him in skill of arms. And now, at last, Val had won to knighthood and could sit, a prince among princes, at the great Table Round in that city of marvel: Camelot! Thus ran Val's thoughts and thus sounded back the echo of his memories while the gulls wheeled overhead and the ship drew ever farther from Britain. Then, of a sudden, Val felt the presence of his father beside him, and of the loyal old warriors, and knew that for them the years in Britain had been spent in dreaming of this day of return to their homeland.

To Britain he himself would return later. Now there was another battle

to be won. Val swung around and faced forward. To Thule! To victory!

Ever north by east the ship sailed, beyond the lands of the Saxon, beyond the nation of the Angles, beyond lands and tribes whose very names were shrouded in mystery. Colder grew the air and angrier the waves, and still they kept to the northward course until rows of jagged cliffs loomed forbiddingly to their right and they knew they were skirting the coast of Scandia. Excitement mounted. All were aware that Thule was not far off now.

At dawn the next day Val was aroused by the hoarse shout of the lookout. There, sparkling in the first light of morning, lay the boats and nets belonging to the friendly Thule fishing village whose men had once helped the exiled king to escape the wrath of Sligon. Then the king ordered the ship turned landward, and boldly Val raised aloft the banner of the Red Stallion under which the king had always fought. From the shore the next instant rose a great cheer of welcome.

Then they landed and sprang ashore. "We have been driven from these shores," the king said. "But now we have returned, nevermore to leave." Then he put a torch to the ship that all might see he burned his only means of flight.

Then followed busy, dangerous days, when swift messengers rode at night into the heart of the country spreading word of the king's return, and telling of his vow to bring freedom and justice for all. Secretly came many of the Thule nobles to pledge loyalty. And the simple peasants came from far and wide to form a ready army. These men Val himself set about training in the hard art of war. Last of all came Sligon's spies, watching, listening, then carrying back to Sligon news that shook the aging tyrant with terror. Finally the hour for action struck! The king gave the orders to march! But scarcely had these orders been given when a messenger galloped up, crying: "Sligon will treat of peace with Prince Valiant if he dare come to the royal castle, alone!"

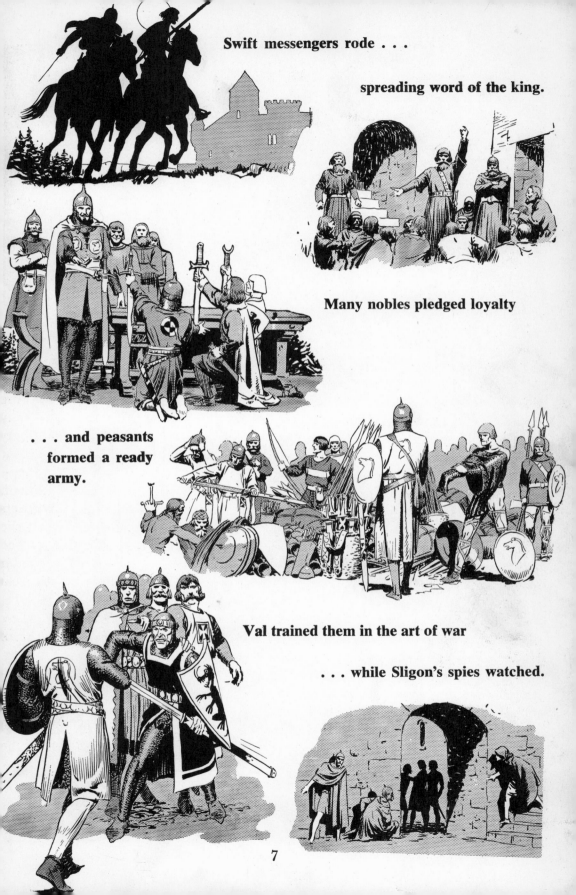

Swift messengers rode . . .

spreading word of the king.

Many nobles pledged loyalty

. . . and peasants formed a ready army.

Val trained them in the art of war

. . . while Sligon's spies watched.

7

Knowing Sligon's treachery, the king's council advised Val to put no faith in the tyrant's guarantee of safety. But Val answered: "I will go!"

8

Then, mounting, Val rode to the towering castle which once had been his own home; and where, now, entering alone, he faced Sligon, surrounded by many well-armed guards. But gone was the tyrant's pride. Before him huddled a broken old man. And, despite his evil, Val pitied Sligon his vanished glory. "I seized Thule by force; by force have I held it. What have I gained? Only hatred, cruelty, distrust and treachery. Go to your father and say — Sligon, the mighty, sits like a beggar on a throne of nettles. Gladly will he barter his stolen crown for your tiny peaceful isle in the fens of Britain."

With this news, Val galloped **back in** all speed to his father's camp. There was no doubting Sligon's desire for escape from the shackles forged by his own tyranny, and his fear of being overwhelmed even by the traitors in his own stronghold.

Great was the relief of the waiting warriors to see Val returning unharmed.

As he drew nearer his father turned to the men around him and said: "Val smiles. Therefore prepare to march. Val was ever one to enjoy a fight. He brings news that Sligon must be fought!"

But Val was shouting: "Peace — peace! Sligon surrenders his throne! There will be no war!"

Pandemonium of joy broke loose in the camp.

Thus was Thule spared the ruin and havoc, the woe and misery of civil war. But Val's father was right. Val would have preferred punishing the tyrant for his crimes. Escape into peace was too good for him. Besides, an unused lance grows rusty and might give other tyrants the wrong idea.

The peace pact with Sligon was nevertheless confirmed, with the tyrant free to leave the shores of Thule unharmed.

So, amid wild rejoicing that spread the length and breadth of the land, the legions under the banner of the Red Stallion took possession of the great fortress where Val's father, and his fathers before him, had ruled with justice and freedom. And as the rightful king re-entered by one gate, so did Sligon at the same moment slip out unnoticed by another, to find what solace he could in the bitter years that remained to him.

10

But royal pomp and ceremony came quickly to an end before hard realities. Corruption, injustices and rascality needed to be plucked out, root and branch. The king gave himself up to the work of returning decency and honor to the warped government of his beloved country.

Meanwhile to Prince Valiant fell a task requiring diplomacy of a different and more stimulating order. Numerous nobles who had thrived well under Sligon's rule of terror refused to acknowledge fealty to the king. Val was

dispatched to bring them into a more reasonable frame of mind.

He at once sought out the most powerful of them in their strongly fortified castles where, living luxuriously behind thick stone walls and amply provided with armed retainers, seasoned warriors and a brawny executioner or two, they smilingly advised the young prince to go chase himself before they ordered the stable varlets to toss him into the moat. Unless, of course, Sir Valiant, Knight of somebody-or-other's Round Table, cared to settle the argument with trial-by-arms?

Settling arguments with trial-by-arms was the approved custom of those rough days.

Only, settling arguments with trial-by-arms was what Val looked forward to in the first place. He accepted the challenges readily — too readily. It made the nobles a mite worried to see how eagerly he grasped his lance and sprang on his charger.

And so, amid the thundering of hoofs, the shattering of lances and the deadly whine of Val's Singing Sword, the obstinate nobles were made to see, as they lay sprawled out on the ground, the very real advantages of peace and quiet under the rule of the king, and the helpful administration of his decidedly charming son.

Happy days for a high-hearted young knight!

Alas, those happy days did not last long. Soon the stock of jarls and earls, insolent and foolhardy enough to flaunt their defiance of Sligon's conqueror, melted away like snow in the sun. In short, Prince Valiant's social calls started a stampede from every castle and stronghold in Thule to swear fealty to the rightful king. Sligon quickly became a forgotten name.

There might be a few murderers, assassins and brigands to tame. But this was hardly work. Thule had settled down to peace and plenty.

Val turned his horse homeward and rode through a sunny, smiling land where farmers and merchants enjoyed a prosperity not often found in those troubled times . . . and Val sighed, thinking again of Britain.

In Britain, too, there was peace and plenty . . . yes, peace for those whose bones creaked with old age, and plenty for those who galloped forth with the spur of youth and sought glorious deeds of arms.

In King Arthur's court no single day passed but that some quest was cried and the Table Round rang loud with the voices of knights and warriors claiming the honor of redressing a wrong though their lives were forfeit in the doing. And there were jousts and tournaments, some splendid, as though at Caerleon; some small, as those mayhap at any path or crossroads. But never a knight

13

in all Britain who wore his armor on a peg — as did now the hearty young warriors of Thule.

Val lost no time upsetting this too cozy state of affairs. Yet he did it as much on his own account as on that of his fellow knights.

Each morning, in the chill of dawn, the palace courtyard echoed with the turbulent clash of arms as Val trained with the other knights, sharpening his skill with sword and dagger. Dangerous exercise it was, and many were the fine knights who limped and hobbled through the palace corridors thereafter, or found it painful making a courtly bow while swathed in bandages.

And Val's disposition improved.

The afternoons, Val spent in the palace gardens, surrounded by maidens of the court, whose enchanting eyes and bewitching lips were more dangerous far against a handsome prince than even the keenest sword and dagger. For love was a serious game, smilingly played with light words and arched glances, with ribbons and scents and shimmering curls. One day the handsome Prince Valiant would be the handsome King Valiant of Thule. And

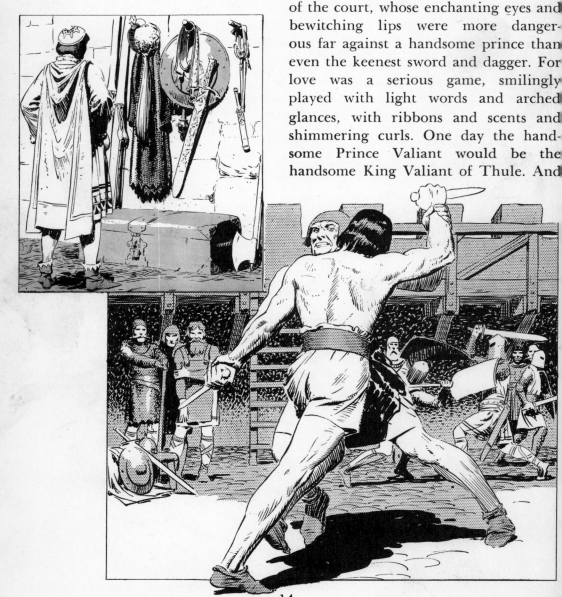

his wife, forsooth, would thereby become a queen. Who could justly blame any of the ambitious fair ones for desiring a husband with such a dazzling future? How were they to know that in his heart he still kept sorrowful vigil for his first love, Ilene, and had room for no other? So Val flirted the golden afternoons away (and what prince or pauper would dare to do less for a pretty face?)—but there he stopped.

The evenings, he spent to his most profit. In his rooms he gathered about him the scholars, painters, poets, travelers, philosophers, and those most skilled in the sciences of the earth and the stars, men of deep learning and nimble wit, who could speak of great things and not forget that they themselves were but the smallest part of that greatness; men with clear, bright words to light up the darkness of the unknown; men who carried the weight of their learning on their shoulders like a beam of morning sunshine, unfrowning.

Thus it was that Val spent his days in Thule.

And each Saturday a tournament was held during which Val, putting aside both love and learning, fought with the sheer joy of the warrior born . . . after which he feasted merrily with the survivors.

It was all ideal, save for one slight detail. Val was bored. So one morning, after a hard workout with his companions, Val, refreshed from his bath, strode up to his father. But even before he could speak, his father stormed: "I know well why you come! No! You will remain in Thule! There will be no more adventuring! You will prepare yourself for the throne!"

To which Val gave answer mockingly: "Prepare for the throne indeed! So my father wishes me to remain at court and learn kingship daintily and sweetly . . . now, just where did I leave my sewing basket?" And Val pirouetted off.

And straightway he doffed the silk of the courtier for the steel of the warrior. "My father forgets," he remarked to his old servant, "that he did precisely the same in his younger days. Must fathers ever forget that they were once sons?" Then he mounted and rode out by the main castle gate, while from a high window the king watched and sighed, and at length smiled, and then silently prayed his son all good fortune in his adventuring even as, in his own youth, it had been so with him.

We go now with Prince Valiant as he travelled far and free seeking whatever adventures it willed Heaven might befall him. And so, with the passing days, he crossed a wide sea in a Viking dragonship to the land of the Danes. Thence he passed along the shores where the fierce Angles built their villages, close to the sea. And there, in a night of gales, his ship dashed itself to pieces, and Val and his beloved war horse were cast on the sharp-toothed rocks. And thus he lay, dazed and sorely bruised. But there was worse. The half-savage villagers, eager for loot, swarmed out of their huts, armed with staves and clubs, and set upon him in all fury, so that he scarce knew which was the more merciless of the two, the raging sea or the brutish men.

Near death Prince Valiant was that night save only that in his desperate plight he drew the Singing Sword and hacked and hewed an open path through the ranks of his pitiless enemies, then mounted his horse and so escaped their clutches, leaving them howling over their dead. Then, after resting in the forest for many days until his wounds healed, and his strength returned to him, he rode on, moving south with the warming sun.

In the low country where the fair-haired Saxons dwelt, a strange adventure befell him. In later years he knew not for certain whether it had truly happened or not—yet it was no dream. It was dusk and he was faint from

hunger and weariness, for he had fought that day against a robber-baron and his men. A storm threatened as, at last, he wiped clean the Singing Sword and sought shelter in a nearby cave. And there, unsmiling, neither bidding him welcome nor barring his way, stood a tall witchwoman by a wine-laden table.

"Your wine is **potent**. My head swims."

The impulsive lad strode into the cave.

"Pardon, lady, do I trespass?" Val asked courteously.

"No, lad," answered the witch. Then she smiled bleakly and proffered Val a goblet of wine. Val drank thirstily, and at once it seemed as if a thin veil had been drawn across his eyes so that all thereafter happened mistily and was already half-forgotten even as it was happening.

"Your wine is potent. My head swims. Where am I and what place is this?"

"This is the Trophy-Room of Time. Here must all men and all things some day come, however unwillingly. Yet none dares enter it before his time."

"I dare any adventure!" And the impulsive lad hitched up his sword belt and strode, somewhat unsteadily, into the deeps of the silent, gloomy cave. A cold, weird glow illuminated this mischancy place and he made out, at the far end, the bent figure of a frail old man seated forlornly on a throne. About him, in great crumbling heaps, lay the dusty wreckage of the treasures wrought by men. From ages beyond all remembering they were, worn and mouldering. Here lay the crowns of kings, mingled with the crutches of beggars and the loot of thieves, and all looked the same at last. Then Val shuddered, for a cold fear suddenly gripped him at the sight of all this hideous ruin. He stopped before the old man. "Who are you?" he asked, trying to keep the growing terror from his voice.

"I am Father Time, and here I store my trophies; the altars of forgotten gods, and the thrones of mighty kings, ageless cities and fortresses unconquerable. I destroy them all, for I am the final victor over all things and no one dare contend with me!"

"I dare!" cried Val; for it seemed to him that the glory of his youth was imperishable. He picked up his senile adversary and flung him among his dusty trophies. But the ancient creature rose and hurled ten years at Val; and Val only laughed for they made him feel more mature. Once more he seized Time and flung him on the heap. And Time gathered up twenty years and sent them hissing on their way. And with them wisdom came and it seemed much better to sit down and arbitrate. But Time smiled an arrogant smile. In rage the middle-aged prince drew his sword and was met with the crushing weight of thirty years! The heavy sword dropped from bony fingers too weak to hold it. How long they struggled in that dim, weird place Val could never afterwards tell. But at last he could struggle no more, and Time cast the remains of what was once a proud prince among the world's dusty relics!

Time hurled ten years at Val.

Once more he seized Time.

They struggled in that dim place. Time cast the remains among the world's dusty relics.

23

Somehow Val managed to lift himself to his feet. Thin, cackling laughter rang in his ears as, with stiffened joints, he staggered out to where the witch-woman stood. Wrinkled hands grasped the goblet she extended and he raised it, trembling, to sunken lips. He drained the cup. The wretched years fell away. Youth returned, and he was once more as he had been!

The next instant he rushed headlong from the cave, leaped upon his waiting horse and galloped away. "What a horrible nightmare! . . . Or was it? How terrible to be old and weak! How good to be young and strong again—I must remember that!" And so, exulting, Val rode far through forest and glade until, in the distance, he glimpsed the sea and turned to ride to it. And suddenly he was startled by hoarse shouts behind him.

Scarcely had he time to spring aside before a line of heavily-laden carts went rumbling past, the beasts being lashed to their utmost speed. The carts were piled high with household goods to which old men and women and children were clinging, the most of them desperately pinched with fright and hunger. Yet they stopped not but careened on.

Pacing beside the foremost of the drivers, Val shouted: "Whence come you and from what manner of terror do you flee?"

And the driver shouted in answer: "Him we flee who is called the Scourge of God—Attila! Make haste! His hordes approach Rome! Flee!"

Then the terror-stricken refugees were gone.

Attila! The Scourge of God! Sweeping out of the limitless East with his hordes! Even before leaving Thule, Prince Valiant had heard tales of this barbaric butcher with his fathomless lust for blood.

Now mighty Rome stood in his path! All Europe might soon be at his mercy!

Thus lost in black thoughts Prince Valiant gave free rein to his mount and at length reached the sea. The sky brooded with storm. Seeing lights shining through the darkness, he directed himself toward them and presently found an inn that promised shelter for the night.

In this inn were gathered sailors from many lands. And as Val, drying himself before the fire, made himself one of their company, he listened in vain for tales of the sea. They spoke only of pleasant lands turned into seas of blood, of wanton and appalling butchery, of thousands and tens of thousands fleeing in shrieking terror before the fierce horsemen of Attila the Hun! And all this while, plodding through the storm, came a wanderer. He entered the inn, haggard, wasted with disease, with deep-set, **burning** eyes. "I bring dire

news! Rome is tottering! Pope Leo pleads with Attila to spare the city! To the south all Europe is in flames! Only the castle of Andelkrag still stands . . . high above the smoke and flames of burning Europe soar the towers of Andelkrag, the unconquerable!"

"Tell me," said Val, "of this unconquerable fortress."

The wanderer's eyes gleamed fever-bright. "To Prince Camoran-of-the-High-Head belongs Andelkrag. Passing great in valor is Camoran, and passing great

is the valor of the companions at his side . . . all those who love beauty
music, poetry and noble deeds. The hordes of Attila beat in waves against the
walls of Andelkrag, but Andelkrag remains unconquered . . . unconquered!"
In consternation then did Prince Valiant see the wanderer clutch his throat as
if choked of air, then fall to the ground, stone dead. The sailors crowded
about in horror, staring at the fallen man. Then one cried: "The Red
Plague! The pestilence! Touch him not!" And so, on the instant, all fled
the accursed place, yet doubting not that the seeds of death were already upon

hem. And for many they were.

Through the night rode Val, and for many days and nights thereafter, thinking always of Castle Andelkrag and of its gallant defender Camoran. Past moldering villages he rode, and fields stripped bare of their harvests, and saw the slain and starved sprawled endlessly along the highways. Yet Val rode on, famished of hunger and grimly watchful. One day, as he drew nearer the castle, a band of foraging Huns swept down on him, brandishing fearful weapons.

Drawing the Singing Sword and spurring his mount into the thick of th
savage horsemen, Val laid about him with such fierceness and valor and prowe
as no barbaric onrush could repel. The foremost of the band galloped upo
him with flailing mace. Val's sword seethed through the air and smote off h
foe's head. Then he hacked and hewed, to the right and left, toppling his foe
off their saddles and down to the ground where he promptly sent them on a
eternal journey; for, once unhorsed, their courage seemed to melt away an
they appeared bewildered and helpless.

At length, seeing that their leader and the most of their comrades lay dead
the survivors dashed off with extreme swiftness and were soon lost to sigh
Now, discovering with joy some joints of an ox tied to the slain leader's horse
Val lit a fire and was soon feasting plentifully.

Andelkrag lay on the far side of a mountain range; and here, picking h
way among the jagged cliffs, Val shaped an uncertain course while keeping
wary watch for Attila's roving avengers. Then suddenly he spied the figur
of a man, half-hidden in a cave. Coming up and seizing him, Val found hir
to be a fugitive shepherd, driven, with many others, into hiding. With tear
of gratitude he accepted Val's proffer of food, then willingly guided him. A
the edge of a cliff he stopped and pointed below.

"Behold! Andelkrag!"

Val picked his way among the jagged cliffs.

Andelkrag! Towers of strength!

Val's heart gladded at the sight of this mighty fortress, the only one left in all burning Europe, pricking like a thorn in Attila's side. From the soaring pinnacles flew gallant Camoran's flags, fluttering gaily. But below, on the ground, around the castle's high walls, Attila's Huns swarmed like an army of ants!

That night, under cover of darkness, Val crept down the slope. Then circling the enemy camp, he let himself quietly into the river which fed the castle's moat. For he had a plan to gain entrance into the castle despite the siege of the all-encompassing enemy.

Val had almost reached the moat when he felt his way blocked by a huge raft piled with dry grass, logs and branches which the enemy was preparing to set ablaze on the morrow in hope of burning away the castle's drawbridge and gate. Watching his moment, Val struck flint on steel. The next instant flames were leaping into the sky and the surprised Huns rushed about in disorder, seeking the culprit. But Val was already crouched under the draw-bridge. And suddenly the drawbridge clanged down as Camoran sortied forth with his men. And while they fell on the confused ranks of the enemy, a mud-spattered knight of King Arthur's Round Table was presenting himself to the astonished guards at the castle's gate.

"Be welcome, youngster!" Camoran laughed when he returned and Andel-krag's gate was shut again. "Fight hard, sing merrily and laugh when you die!" Then he toasted Prince Valiant before all his joyful company. For all were joyful, even the wounded and the ladies and maidens who tended them.

"Be welcome, youngster!" Camoran laughed.

Then he toasted Prince Valiant.

For all were joyful, even the wounded and ladies who tended them.

35

And so, with death hovering over them all, the weeks went by. And ye
Camoran and his company let nothing dampen their high spirits. The Huns were
like demons in the fury of their onslaughts. But the defenders of Andelkrag
sang battle-chants and laughed as they fought. Each passing moment counted
as one precious moment less in the shortening lives of the gallant men and

their ladies within the stout bastions of Andelkrag; but each small moment was as a lifetime crowded with zest. With them a whole age was coming to an end, perhaps the most high-hearted, the most dedicated to beauty, the most truly wise the world would ever know. But end it would, if end it must, gloriously, before barbaric darkness closed in.

When darkness fell and the attacks diminished, Camoran and his fellowship dined nobly, with songs and gay music; and highly did they vaunt the lilting voice and merry throbbing lute of the young prince who had come to fight, and perchance to die, by their side.

Meanwhile, the tireless Huns filled in the moat, then brought up huge, lurching siege-towers. But with grapples the defenders sent them crashing to the earth. Then monstrous, roofed battering-rams thudded day and night until Andelkrag's stone wall crumbled—but when the overconfident foe rushed into the breach it was only to find themselves facing a stronger inner wall, and under a hail of laughter and boulders from above.

The battering-rams thudded day and night.

The overconfident foe found themselves facing an inner wall.

Meanwhile, inside the fortress life went on gaily. Val wondered how long this lavishness could last. "Camoran," he said, "should we not banquet more frugally?" To which Camoran replied, "Would you have barbarians alter the ways of living at Andelkrag? Sir Valiant, we will live, love, fight and die like gentlemen!"

And so, as the days wore into weeks and the weeks into months, still Andelkrag remained unconquered, within and without. The scarred warriors on the battlements were fewer now but undaunted. And beneath the battlements the enemy lay sprawled in heaps.

Then at last the dreaded day came. Andelkrag's defenders gathered about the great table and saw that of food and drink there was no more!

Smiling, Camoran arose. "Tomorrow we will do that which we have to do. Tomorrow the barbarians will rule the world. But we, the last of the warrior-troubadours, will die as we have lived, gaily and free. We have loved this world, and this world has loved us. Now our time draws near. Tomorrow it is hail and farewell. Come, Val, let us have song and merriment!"

41

Next morning at the first light of dawn, all the vast treasure of Andelkrag from generations untold was gathered into iron-bound oaken chests and carried into the lofty hall, then lowered into a deep vault beneath the floor of the castle.

This being done, the graceful, high-spirited ladies bade all adieu, and slowly, one by one, mounted the tower stairway, not speaking further nor

glancing behind. And they were gone. Then Camoran called for a torch and himself applied the flame that would bring roof and walls of great Andelkrag crashing down.

As the tongues of fire leaped up in red hunger, Val cried: "The ladies, Camoran—they never descended from the tower!"

Terrible to behold was the face of Camoran as he replied, "Our ladies do not choose to fall into the hands of those who wait outside!"

Peering through the loophole into the wild faces of Attila's men, Prince Valiant understood why death was welcome.

Little time remained for what was yet to be done. Scarcely speaking one to another, the defenders put themselves in readiness for the final fight. Then quietly, calmly all followed behind their leader into a wide chamber deep under Andelkrag's lowest dungeon. And now, at a word from Camoran, an immense stone block was hoisted from the floor, and Val saw revealed a secret passage leading beneath the moat, thence out to where the enemy stood.

"When we shall all meet again I know not," Camoran said. All clasped in a last embrace of fellowship. Then Val drew his Singing Sword. "Would that Attila himself waited outside," he said. Then through the dark passage they filed, and fearful was the gleam of their eyes.

43

The tunnel's mouth was blocked by a massive boulder. But they hurled their strength against it and it yielded. Out into the blinding sunshine they leaped, shouting their battle cry. A dozen paces off the barbarians turned to meet the charging, mail-clad warriors.

Through the screaming hordes the men of Andelkrag hacked a crimson road; then, when they could advance no further, stood and fought until they

ank beneath the weight of the enemy. And so Camoran fell at last, and with
him many another of his gay comrades. But within the flaming circle of the
dread Singing Sword, Prince Valiant fought on. And then he too was borne
down and lay stretched upon the earth.

It was night when Val struggled once more to his feet and by the flare of
torches saw the Huns slithering off like a wounded serpent through the narrow

mountain pass into Hungary. The siege was ended.

Still blazing was Andelkrag, and casting a fitful glow over the field of battle. Val moved slowly among the dead, scanning the faces. And there, prone atop a mound of his enemies, lay the body of him for whom Val searched.

With Camoran in his arms, Val staggered to the tunnel's mouth and bore his heavy burden under the moat, then trudged step by step up to the top of the eastern tower. "Your beloved Andelkrag, still unconquered, shall be your bier, Camoran!" And Val gave him to the devouring flames.

Descending, Val made his way wearily high up in the hillside, away from the Hun-infested pass. Near the summit he paused and saw the castle walls come crashing down, a smoldering ruin now which the ivy would one day cover. And at the edge of a dark pool, Val sank down and slept.

When he stirred again the noonday sun was sparkling on the jeweled hilt of the Singing Sword, while across the pool, two shrewd eyes watched him.

Val sank down and slept.
Two shrewd eyes watched him.

Unmindful of his stealthy watcher Val arose, then stepped to the edge of the pool. He unclasped his sword and removed his suit of mail. The cool, clear water so soothed his hurts that he failed to notice the crouching figure creeping closer . . . until a dislodged pebble came rattling down and splashed close by. Val whirled around. Then came swift action. An instant later the attacker

was being calmly drowned. Then curiosity got the better of Val. He dumped him on the bank and demanded, "Why?"

"Why not?" grinned the rascal. "I'd kill my own grandmother for the gems in that sword you now hold at my throat! I am Slith, thief, juggler, actor, singer and magician. I live by my wits and every man is my enemy. I am really not worth killing . . . I hope."

Val laughed at this impudence and kicked him to his feet. Whereupon Slith grateful, led him to his camp, and a breakfast, and a shave. "Come, Sir Valiant the wide world lies before us! You shall see how we travel on our wits!" So

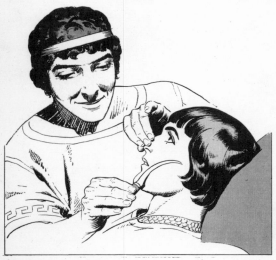 

he packed his faithful ass Socrates and they set forth. "Look!" cried Slith presently. "Huns! Observe how I part those barbaric boobies from their loot!" And from above Val, scowling, watched.

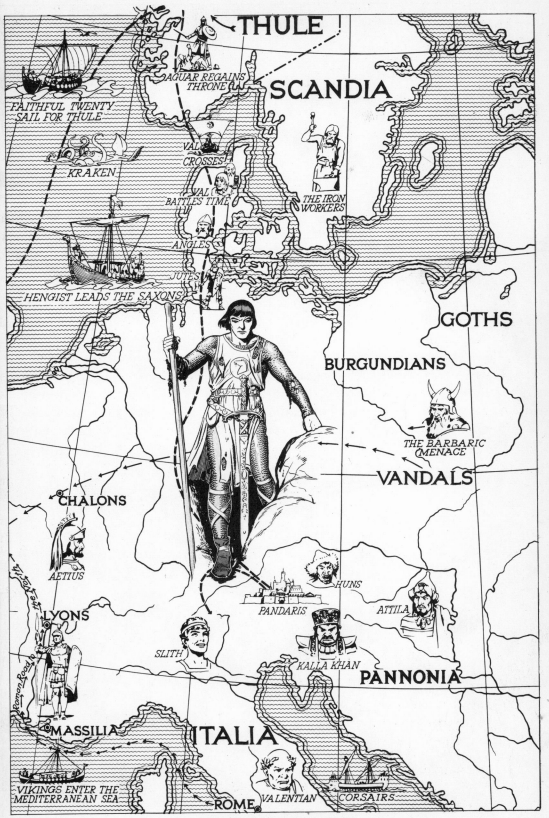

THULE

SCANDIA

FAITHFUL TWENTY SAIL FOR THULE

AGUAR REGAINS THRONE

KRAKEN

VAL CROSSES!

THE IRON WORKERS

VAL BATTLES TIME

ANGLES

JUTES

GOTHS

HENGIST LEADS THE SAXONS

BURGUNDIANS

THE BARBARIC MENACE

VANDALS

CHALONS

AETIUS

LYONS

the Nor..

Roman Roads

MASSILIA

SLITH

PANDARIS

HUNS

ATTILA

KALLA KHAN

PANNONIA

ITALIA

VIKINGS ENTER THE MEDITERRANEAN SEA

ROME

VALENTIAN

CORSAIRS

" . . . the wide world lies before us."

But even as Val stood, leaning on his staff, fury surged up in him at the sight of the detested barbarians. Then once again the sun flashed on the jeweled hilt of the Singing Sword and the Huns glanced up with greed.

"Nay!" argued Slith. "The gems are false, mere colored pebbles!" But the Huns were already swarming up the hillside, weapons drawn. Slith fitted a rock in his sling and waited, fearful of Val's life. But it hung unused as Slith stood in amaze. For his companion seemed to whirl like a hurricane in a field of chaff. Sword and staff were everywhere at once, slashing, flailing tripping, killing.

He whirled like a hurricane in a field of chaff. Sword and staff were everywhere.

When the last living Hun, dodging both sword and staff, fled down the hillside, Slith ran up to his companion in joy. "But Sir Valiant," he said soberly a moment later, "take my professional advice and conceal that jeweled sword-hilt and scabbard. You fight like a demon, yet is it not foolhardy to tempt every brigand in these mountains to murder you?"

"Including you, Slith?" laughed Val. Nevertheless he conceded that there was wisdom in Slith's words, and forthwith he fashioned a cover and binding for both hilt and scabbard. He deemed it wise also, considering the number of Huns at large, to disguise himself in Hun's clothing; and watched, therefore, until he discerned a Hun chieftain leading a troop. "Yonder goes my new garb," he remarked to Slith. "Admirable," approved Slith, "but how will you

remove the Hun from inside it?" Val smiled. Noting where the Huns set up camp for the night, he selected a large pine overhanging the trail. He hacked it almost through, then propped it up with a stout limb.

At dawn the Hun chieftain came riding jauntily up. Val dislodged the prop. Down crashed the great tree, cutting the chieftain off from the rest of his men. Then Val sprang nimbly forward to oust the Hun from his clothes.

But Val's victim was being swept down the trail on his terror-stricken mount. Meanwhile, the fallen tree had spread indescribable confusion among the horsemen to the rear. At this moment a second man broke through the tangle of branches and, with drawn sword, Val sprang from the rocks above, quickly dispatching him and possessing himself of his horse. Then, whirling about, he galloped after his intended boots, tunic, gauntlets and helmet. Closing in on the chieftain's left, Val put him to awkward disadvantage in the sword-clash that followed, and soon had his hapless wardrobe choosing between nakedness or death. But now Slith and his ever-faithful long-eared friend Soc-

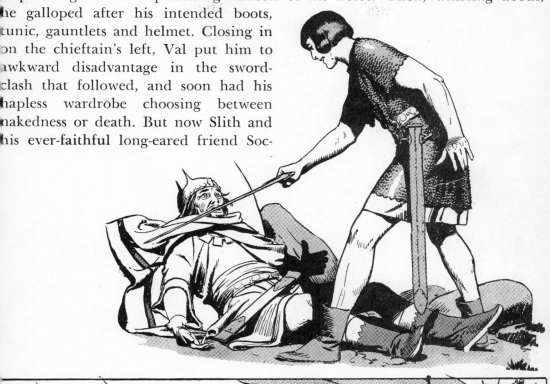

Slith came with no fewer than fift Huns in pursuit

"No! You're going the wrong way! cried Slith.

ates were filling the air with their terrified shouting and braying. Val looked
up. The crafty rogue Slith was indeed in grave peril. For he was now sprinting
down the rocks toward Val with no fewer than fifty furious Huns in blood-
thirsty pursuit. At his side Socrates was bounding like a mountain goat. Though
the Huns were close on their heels, they were fortunately all afoot. And here
Val perceived the great weakness of the Hun warrior. Accustomed to fighting
mounted, he was slow, clumsy, almost helpless as a fighter when deprived of
his horse. But to Slith now, the pursuing Huns seemed more ferocious than
a pack of wolves.

What had happened was this. The fallen pine had been a barrier for the

Hun horses. But the Huns themselves, dismounting, had come tearing out.

Val was already mounted on the Hun chieftain's horse. At his call Slith,
on reaching Val, fairly vaulted into the saddle of the other horse. Instantly
Val set off at a gallop up the mountain path toward the fallen tree. "No!
You're going the wrong way!" cried Slith in anguish. But Val motioned him
to follow. At the fallen tree two Huns were busy clearing away the obstruction.
They glanced up—saw two swords flash . . . and saw no more forever. On
the far side of the fallen tree were all the mounts and pack animals belonging
to the troop, gathered there until the way should be free. Yelling and waving,
Val sent them stampeding up the path, and thus left isolated in the hills half
a hundred Hun horsemen, without horses.

They
reached
the
valley
floor.

They
blocked
one
of
the
ends
with
trees.

After some little time, **finding** themselves secure from attack, Val slowed the animals, then drove them leisurely off the trail and down through the wooded slopes until they reached the valley floor. This they crossed. Then, coming on a grassy, high-walled gorge, they let the animals enter it and blocked off one of the ends with a pile of trees. Across the other end they made their camp.

"Slith, my brave thief," said Val, smiling as he gazed at the plunder now contentedly nibbling the moist grass, "you must acknowledge in all honesty, if I may use the word, that between us, I am the greater brigand."

"Sir Valiant," replied Slith readily, "you crush my pride and shame me

into the petty pilferer that I am. The pity of it is that your brigandage is only a side line. But let us take careful stock of the extent of your haul." The pack animals were thereupon relieved of their bulging sacks and the contents examined.

Of gold and other precious loot there was wealth aplenty. But of this Prince Valiant, despite Slith's gasps of joy, took slight account except to remark that all should some day be returned to the owners from whom the Huns had stolen it. But his eyes blazed with satisfaction on seeing the store of weapons. "Enough for a small army!" Then he grew thoughtful until at length he said, "For nearly six years the Hun has robbed and pillaged Europe. Slith! I need some fighting men—refugees or bandits, I care not which—so long only as they hate the Hun and are bold enough to rob and pillage him! Find these men for me!"

Val had found warriors.

62

Far up in the remote valleys they came on small tilled fields all but con-
cealed from sight; though search as they would, they could find no sign of
dwellings. "Yet people there must be, somewhere," said Val. Slith nodded and
drew from the pouch across Socrates' saddle a curved horn, then sounded a
shrill call familiar only to the peasants and shepherds of the region.

Almost at once they heard an answering call from among the rocks and
trees and saw two shepherds peering cautiously from a high ledge. Val hailed
them. "We are friends! We plunder the Huns! Bring ten brave fighting men
and I will share with them all the food they can carry off on their backs!" The
shepherds withdrew, and a short time later came down with a handful of sus-
picious comrades. True to his word, Val let each man bear off all he could
carry of food and supplies. When they had gone, Slith groaned, "We shall
never see them again. This is useless extravagance!" To which Val retorted,
"Nay, every one will be back! For, mark you Slith, no man is ever satisfied.
And more will come as the news spreads!"

And right he was! Before the day was out, a crowd of wild, stalwart but
half-famished men had come from their caves in the hills and were clamoring
for food. "Tonight," said Val, "I go to rob the Hun again! Now is his turn
come to bleed and starve, even as he has bled and starved you! Who will follow
me?" A fierce cheer went up. Val had found warriors.

Oh, the joy that filled the heart of Prince Valiant as once again he rode at the head of a troop of fighting men! Some were peasants, some shepherds, but the most were seasoned warriors driven in defeat from great castles like Andelkrag, and dispersed. For them too was there joy in being united in burning hatred under an able captain, with weapons of vengeance provided by the foe himself.

At the edge of the broad valley of the mountain pass, Val halted his troop, then posted sentinels to spy from the high surrounding cliffs. Below spread a well-watered meadow in which customarily those Huns who crossed the pass made camp for the night. But no Huns were in the meadow now.

Then, at dusk, Slith, watching near Prince Valiant, sounded a low warning note on his horn. Down from the snow-covered peaks and into the meadow came their prey, a Hun caravan heavy with the loot of months of raiding. The Hun warriors were presently seen pitching their tents. But for many that slept that night there was to be no awakening.

Soundlessly Val and his men approached the dark encampment. Then with wild yells they thundered down. Scarce were the bewildered barbarians aware of their peril than it was upon them. In an instant all was panic and havoc. But worst was a young warrior garbed like a Hun chieftain, whose princely sword clove among them no less untiring and remorseless than that of the

great Attila himself. And before they could collect themselves in the fearful scattering confusion, their baggage animals were reloaded, their loot stolen, their mounts seized—and the marauders were clattering off into the darkness as swiftly as they had come. And bitter it was for the plunderers to be plundered and for horsemen to lose their horses.

Dawn found the raiders safe once more in the hidden side valley, tasting for the first time in six woeful years the triumph of conquerors.

As before, in dismissing them, Val granted to each man the right to take as much of the plunder as he could carry, knowing shrewdly that the news of his victory and his open-handed generosity would spread far and wide throughout the hills and bring more fighting auxiliaries to his side, men hungering for food and thirsting for revenge. And this indeed was as it happened. And as his troop grew in size and strength, so did the scope of his plans against the Hun widen.

Through spies Val was informed that his foes, becoming wary, no longer moved in small bands across the pass, but gathered themselves in large, well

protected numbers before crossing. This news pleased Val. Great caravans meant great loot; while large numbers were of dubious value within the narrow confines of the mountain pass. They could be tricked.

Accordingly, with the faithful Socrates carrying a week's provisions in his saddle-pouch, Val set out with Slith to make a careful study of the mountain pass and its surroundings; and found, after diligent search, an easily defended gorge stemming just off it. And here Val, on summoning his auxiliaries to the spot, caused a strong barricade to be mounted.

When this was done Val drew his chosen leaders about him, and over a miniature of the mountain area cunningly wrought by Slith, rehearsed them in the details of his stratagem against the next great Hun caravan that should cross over the pass. So all was arranged beforehand. It was known that a caravan was now forming on the far side of the pass and must soon move.

Then came word that the Hun caravan had at last started. It was formidably protected. At its head rode a vanguard of a thousand mounted warriors. Guarding its rear were five hundred more warriors, likewise mounted. The baggage animals and a few drivers thus moved in the middle closely linked between two bodies of strongly-armed, swift troops. There seemed little reason to suppose the raiders would dare to attack.

In contrast to these great numbers at the enemy's command, Prince Valiant had no more than three hundred auxiliaries, including old men and boys. Nor were there enough horses for all.

And now, as the strong Hun caravan moved across the winding valley of the pass, Val's forces were disposed as follows. His mounted auxiliaries were stationed ahead on the pass and out of sight of the Huns, there to wait until they heard a prearranged signal. Hidden in the narrow gorge, with the barricade lifted, were his foot soldiers; while he himself, with his officers and Slith, watched atop the high wall of the gorge for the moment when the vanguard

69

of the caravan winding along the narrow pass should have moved up, leaving the baggage animals passing directly before the mouth of Val's gorge.

That moment now arrived. Slith sounded a signal on his horn.

Instantly Val's mounted auxiliaries waiting ahead on the pass, galloped out of hiding and swept straight down toward the Hun vanguard. Onward

they came, shouting. Then, when quite close and seeing, as if for the first time, the formidable strength of that vanguard, they abruptly veered off the pass and sped across the broad valley. The entire Hun vanguard at once set after them in savage pursuit. In a moment pursuers and pursued were far off. It was not until the Huns reached the opposite side of the valley that they caught up with the "raiders", and then they were wild with rage to discover that they consisted of old men and young boys. Now, belatedly, they realized they had been tricked away from the caravan for a purpose which they could only too readily guess. Without an instant's delay they raced back to the pass.

They were already too late!

For no sooner had the Hun vanguard been decoyed off than Val and his men dashed out of the gorge and took charge of the baggage animals. The few drivers set up a shrieking. The Hun warriors forming the rearguard, which was strung out in a long straggling line to the rear, endeavored to come to their aid. But this was not to be accomplished on the narrow, winding pass. A handful of Val's men dispatched them or forced them off the edge as fast as they came.

While the Hun rearguard was thus kept at bay, and their vanguard had not yet returned, all the baggage animals were driven deep inside the gorge and safely past the open barricade. On the pass a great pile of debris was avalanched from the hillside to impede and harass the remaining warriors of the rearguard and keep them from immediately following. Then Val's men scurried back into the gorge and the heavy barricade was closed.

It was not in Val's reckoning that the outraged barbarians would calmly suffer the loss of their supplies and fabulously rich plunder. He therefore braced his men for the expected onslaught. It was not long in coming. The Hun chieftain, he who had led the vanguard and allowed himself to be outwitted, soon reassembled all his warriors, then roared for the barricade to be stormed and the feeble band of defenders put to the sword.

But storming the barricade head on proved costly and futile for the Hun horsemen. Standing in their saddles, they fought fiercely. They were relentlessly hewed down from above. They drew back to consider new tactics.

Presently, from within the enclosure, Prince Valiant saw a considerable number of them dismounting and swarming toward the steep rocky walls that rose at each end of the barricade. These warriors now started to claw their way up, hoping thereby to climb above and around the barricade and leap on the defenders inside while their remaining companions continued the assault from the front.

For awhile Val's men welcomed the climbers with boulders hurled down on them from the topmost ridges of the two flanking walls. But the maimed and slain barbarians were at once replaced by others. When at last it became plain that through sheer force of numbers the Huns would ultimately succeed in their maneuver, Val put torches to the barricade and swiftly retreated through the gorge with all his men and the captured caravan, leaving the Huns to cool their fury before a raging wall of fire.

Reaching the far end of the gorge, Val divided his men into small groups, charging each to take a part of the caravan and return to the hidden valley by different and scattered routes. Thus men and booty melted into the forested hills while Val with a few archers remained to watch from a height how the

73

enemy progressed when the way was cleared.

When at length the heavy-timbered barricade shuddered to the ground in sparking ashes, the Hun galloped past it into the dark gorge, searching frantically for some sign of their stolen caravan. They found nothing.

Up and down the broad valley they prowled, hungering less as the day wore on for their precious loot than for the priceless supplies of food and drink. For where should they find that which to eat in a land they themselves had laid waste? And even as, in the mocking twilight, they charged at shadows and slashed at mist there came stinging flights of arrows down on them from the cliffs. Then the Hun chieftain lifted his arms and called down the wrath of his thundering gods òn Prince Valiant. And in the end, swearing vengeance, the Huns departed over the pass.

That night Val and his band of Hun-hunters, for so they now began naming themselves, held a feast of victory and toasted their absent hosts.

And in far-off ancient Pannonia, now Hungary, the Great Khan of the Huns learned of the theft of his caravan, and his face grew black with rage.

The Great Khan's face
grew black with rage.

75

Then the Great Khan, brooding that Prince Valiant, if left alive, might set off the spark to throw all Europe in flaming revolt, summoned before him the commander of his armies, grim-faced Karnak the Ferocious. To him he spoke, saying, "We suffer none to oppose us, neither great nor small." Then he told of Prince Valiant, knight of Britain's king, who with a rabble of emboldened warrior-thieves played havoc with the caravans crossing the mountain pass. "Clear the pass. Fortify it. And in two moons return with the head of Prince Valiant."

Karnak bowed and would have gone. But the Great Khan pointed to two

stakes that stood before the entrance to his tent. "On the first, Karnak, rests the head of a defeated general. The second, as yet unadorned, is for the head of Prince Valiant . . . or your own!" For an instant Karnak's lifted hand touched his throat, then he was gone.

Karnak lost little time gathering an army and setting forth. It was his head against Prince Valiant's, and his own he meant resolutely to keep. Nor had he any misgivings that the knight could long escape his iron claws. It was one thing to dart off with the horses, loot and supplies of a column of weary troops; it would be otherwise to face a legion of hardened veterans before whom the armies of a score of nations from Mongolia to the Mediterranean had already fled in terror. No, the head of Karnak, lean, cunning and cruel eyed, was safe.

On the plains below the pass Prince Valiant saw the Huns building an immense camp, amply laid out and strongly fortified. The barbarians then were no longer depending on the mere terror of their name to keep their victims from rising against them. In this very show of Hun strength Val seemed to see an open display of monstrous fear and weakness.

Meanwhile the reports of Val's resounding victories brought daily more men to his side. Crafty Valentinian III sent five hundred knights from Rome, well-armed and mounted. From Spain came a thousand hard-fighting Visigoths.

77

But best of all, from King Arthur's court arrived two battle-scarred knights. Val recognized them from afar. "Sir Tristram! Sir Gawain!" Gawain, merry as always, explained why they had come. "Tristram seeks to forget his love for the fair Isolde. I seek to forget I have no loves at all!"

Thus, happily, the three companions strode arm-in-arm to Val's tent. Under Val's hand a great army was being united. Heavy were the burdens of planning shrewdly and wisely. But of fighting there was plenty, too.

Prince Valiant's warriors held the pass. Yet hardly a day passed when parties of Huns from Karnak's camp did not spring out from ambush. Then with mighty Tristram and Gawain beside him Val forsook cool planning for hot and deadly action. "I'm glad we came," said Gawain.

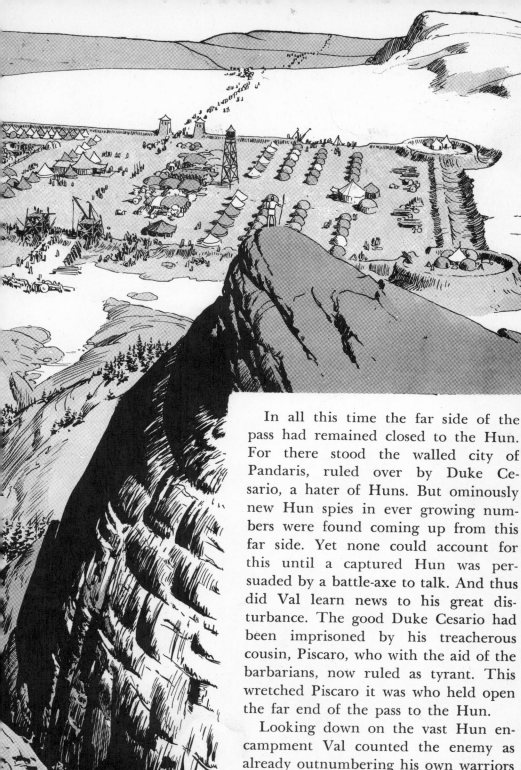

In all this time the far side of the pass had remained closed to the Hun. For there stood the walled city of Pandaris, ruled over by Duke Cesario, a hater of Huns. But ominously new Hun spies in ever growing numbers were found coming up from this far side. Yet none could account for this until a captured Hun was persuaded by a battle-axe to talk. And thus did Val learn news to his great disturbance. The good Duke Cesario had been imprisoned by his treacherous cousin, Piscaro, who with the aid of the barbarians, now ruled as tyrant. This wretched Piscaro it was who held open the far end of the pass to the Hun.

Looking down on the vast Hun encampment Val counted the enemy as already outnumbering his own warriors by twenty to one. "To be attacked from both sides of the pass at once will end in our disaster. The pass must be again shut. I will go to Pandaris!"

To this perilous intent Val's war-council voiced strong protests, but shortly thereafter, accompanied by none but Slith and long-eared Socrates, he crossed the icy, wind-driven summit. Then, timing his descent with the coming of night, he safely passed several small Hun encampments clustered about the far side

of the pass. Being now at the outskirts of the walled city he did not enter at once, however, but proceeded first to the villa of a wealthy merchant named Guido to whom he had been recommended by one of his warriors. This Guido was a loyal friend to the imprisoned duke though, for his own security, he pretended otherwise. Here Val and Slith were given good hospitality, and learned more of how matters stood within the city walls.

"Duke Cesario was well-loved by his people," the merchant said, "but took scant notice until too late of his cousin Piscaro's treasonable dealings with the Huns. Piscaro is weak and vicious, a cruel tyrant. He keeps himself surrounded by the Huns who fill the city and maintain him in power. None dares raise his voice against him or the Huns, for the merest whisper overheard by a spy ends in hideous torture and death.

"Nonetheless," the merchant continued, lowering his voice even in his own home, "there are 'Liberators' who meet and work in secret to free the city. You will not know them. But they will know you."

The next morning, wearing the guise of country peddlers, they approached the city nestling at the foot of the mountains. They passed through the gates unmolested and were soon making their way along the arched streets toward the tyrant's palace. They did not fail to notice the silent, brooding people nor the armed Hun guards who grimly lined the street.

Of a sudden there came the blare of trumpets, the wild clattering of hooves and the shouts of the soldiery. "Piscaro rides forth from his palace!" Slith cried out in warning. The next instant Piscaro's guards rushed through the street beating back with their rods all who were slow in clearing the way. "Kneel

in the dust, sons of dogs—His Highness approaches!"

Prince Valiant reluctantly moved aside with the others. But when those beside him dropped to their knees, he remained upright, feeling that such servility ill became a king's son and a Knight of the Round Table. "Kneel, Sir Valiant!" implored Slith, growing frantic with fear as the hoofbeats drew nearer. On either side of Val the citizens were whispering, "Kneel, sir! A terrible death awaits those who offend Duke Piscaro!"

The tyrant now appeared riding in the midst of his soldiers, foppishly breathing the fragrance of a scented tassel as though to keep from being assailed by the same air breathed by his kneeling subjects. Prince Valiant, standing to his full height, grimaced contemptuously. "The beast he rides on is worthy of more honor than this stable clown who rules as duke!"

The somber eye of the tyrant fell on the lone erect figure among all those kneeling. He halted, flushed with rage. "Break his legs that he may hereafter find it easier to kneel," he commanded his guards.

"Thanks for reminding me of my legs!" shouted Val, and promptly used them. Down one street and up another he dodged, pursued by the guards with drawn swords. He would in the end have thrown them off had not ill luck led him into a blind street from which there was no outlet.

Seeing no means of escape Val drew his dagger and whirled around when
suddenly a powerful arm jerked him inside a doorway. He would have plunged
his dagger but that a voice whispered, "Liberators! . . . Come, Prince Valiant!"
With that the stranger led the way into a dim room and, crouching, entered
a fireplace. Val followed—climbed in the darkness—and emerged into the adjoining house. And here assembled were the men of freedom of whom Guido had
spoken, offering friendship and a hiding place from the tyrant's assassins.

Val found the Liberators, like all bold men of good will, ready for any sacrifice against their oppressors. "I myself will kill Piscaro. Cesario must be restored to rule. The Hun must be driven from the city and the pass shut." But to kill Piscaro Val had first to get near him. To this end he once more donned Hun garb, then bidding his friends prepare the people for armed uprising, he strode forth. Scarce had he taken a dozen steps before he was recognized and violently seized and forthwith dragged off to Piscaro.

Piscaro gleamed with hate. "Who are the Liberators? Name them!" But Val, remaining mute, was cast in a cell. And there, through a window, he glimpsed the haggard Duke Cesario . . . but knew better than to talk while Piscaro's spy listened outside. And so at last came Piscaro again and ordered torture.

Then was Val put to the rack while Piscaro looked on in glee, until there sounded a hideous crack and, in agony, Val screamed he would name the Liberators, but only to Piscaro alone. So Val was laid on a cot more dead than alive and Piscaro poised his knife. "We are alone! Speak!" On the instant his broken victim shot out an arm and choked off the tyrant's shriek.

Piscaro poised his knife. "Speak!"

Val choked off the tyrant's shriek.

Into the crushing blow that followed went the whole of Val's loathing
When Piscaro returned to consciousness, he was no longer Piscaro. His curl
had been shorn, his face begrimed, and Val's rags substituted for his finery
And in Val, sitting in perfumed elegance shaving himself with a dagger, the
terrified tyrant saw himself as he had once been! "Your rack broke no bones,"
taunted Val. "I just clicked my teeth and snapped my fingers." Then, as he

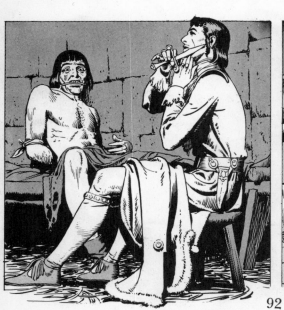

tood to go, Val whispered in through the window to the adjoining cell, "Be
of good cheer, Cesario! You will soon be freed!" Outside the dungeon door the
black-hooded master torturer and his assistant nodded obediently as the mincing
figure passed; then they returned to finish with the prisoner.

On reaching the tyrant's rooms, Val at once summoned the captain of the
guard and commanded that Duke Cesario be brought up to him in chains for
questioning. This being done and the doors to the rooms bolted, Val unchained
the duke and both joyfully thanked Providence. Then they set about planning
how to escape unscathed from the palace infested as it was with the tyrant's
armed retainers. "I have it!" Val cried suddenly. "We cannot go to our friends,
but we can speedily bring our friends to us!" With that he cautioned Cesario
to make a pretense of being chained, then called in the guards. "I have forced
my dear cousin Cesario to betray the names of all the Liberators! Arrest them!
Lock them all in the armory, unharmed that I may put them to torture, one

by one! Make haste now!''

"Ah, Sir Valiant," said Cesario when they were alone again, "I see now the excellence of your plan. In no other way can our friends enter this stronghold short of assaulting it. And then might they as well as ourselves be slain, and our cousin Piscaro and his Huns win their greatest triumph."

That night, while the city slept, Piscaro's men moved through the dark streets. Then brutally they tore the Liberators from their homes, searched them for weapons and bound them with chains. And for these brave men and their dear ones this was the final treachery and the last departure, for not one among them but knew that death waited at the end of this journey. And so by daybreak they were herded through the gate of the tyrant's palace like cattle marked for slaughter, and driven inside the gloomy, echoing armory. The massive doors were clanged shut and bolted. And there they were left shouting with bitter courage: "Death to Piscaro! Death to the Huns! We die for freedom!"

From the window above the courtyard Prince Valiant and Cesario watched, and their hearts went out to their loyal friends. But no hand could they yet lift to spare them this cruelty for fear of prematurely disclosing the entire plot and thereby bringing fatal consequences on them all. Indeed, the most pressing problem still remained unresolved. How was Duke Cesario to be freed without exciting suspicion among Piscaro's soldiers? Unexpectedly the solution was presented to Val by the timely arrival of the master of the dungeons. Val per-

eived, as this wretch stood before him, that in figure and pallor he bore a near ikeness to the haggard Cesario. An idea came to him.

Gloating as he addressed him whom he fancied was Piscaro, the torturer aid: "Your Excellency will relish knowing that we have dispatched Prince Valiant most valiantly. In the end his mind gave way. He screamed in dying hat he was Piscaro—and that you were Prince Valiant."

Val's eyes were blazing. "Fool! He spoke the truth!" And in those words

the torturer heard his doom. He turned to flee. He was too late. And thus i
turned out that Duke Cesario became suddenly the master of the dungeon
while the former holder of that dubious honor found himself elevated t
ducal rank and chained to the wall. Then Cesario, smiling wryly, pondere
the irony of fortune that gave to an open-hearted young knight the seemin
character of tyranny, and made of himself, a wise and merciful ruler, th
wretched master of misery and despair.

Now we return to Slith, who day after day wandered the streets of Pandari
vainly seeking some word of his friend's fate; then dropped down at last on th
cathedral steps, utterly without hope. And in Val's camp on the mountai
pass there was also concern at his long absence. So Hulta, the messenger, mounte
and came swiftly to Pandaris to see for himself how matters stood.

It was not long before Hulta came upon the dejected Slith. "Hulta, m
comrade," said Slith mournfully, "our chieftain is a prisoner of Piscaro.

BESARO

VONDERMAN

Then Hulta galloped back to the camp with this dismal news; and in fury all would have stormed Piscaro's palace. "Nay," said Hulta, "for should we leave the pass undefended, all Prince Valiant's work is undone." And so, reluctantly, all let this wise counsel prevail—except that Hulta, biding his time, rode back secretly to Pandaris thinking that he alone would not be missed—and by surprise met on the way Sir Gawain, Sir Tristram, Vonderman, De Gatin and Besaro, all of whom had the same idea in mind.

DE GATIN

HULTA

But of the coming of these welcome reinforcements, Val as yet knew nothing. Meanwhile, deeming everything to be in readiness for the final stroke, what with Duke Cesario and himself able to pass among the enemy unrecognized, and the Liberators already within the stronghold and stirred up to a pitch of frenzy against their persecutors, Val cautioned the duke to keep his face half-hidden in the folds of his black hood, then called for the palace guards. They presented themselves at once. "To the armory!" commanded Val.

Convinced that the moment was now come for slaughter of the Liberators, Piscaro's guards marched briskly across the courtyard escorting Prince Valiant and Duke Cesario whom, had they recognized either, they would willingly have slaughtered first. At the armory doors Val called a halt, then spoke to the captain of the guard. "Wait here. I will go inside with my executioner and have some sport with these traitors. I may amuse myself by slaying a few. Guard the doors well and let no one enter until I call."

No sooner were Val and the duke inside than they dropped their disguises and revealed themselves to their overjoyed friends. Then swiftly and silently the captives were loosed of their chains and from the armory stores given weapons and armor. When all were thus arrayed for combat, Prince Valiant threw open the doors. Then did the guards in dismay find themselves facing not a band of helpless prisoners, but a phalanx of fierce warriors led by a young knight and a grim-faced executioner who bore an exact likeness to Prince Valiant and Duke Cesario. When the guards were disposed of, the Liberators stormed into the great hall of the palace and, with equal fury, disposed of Piscaro's courtiers and retainers.

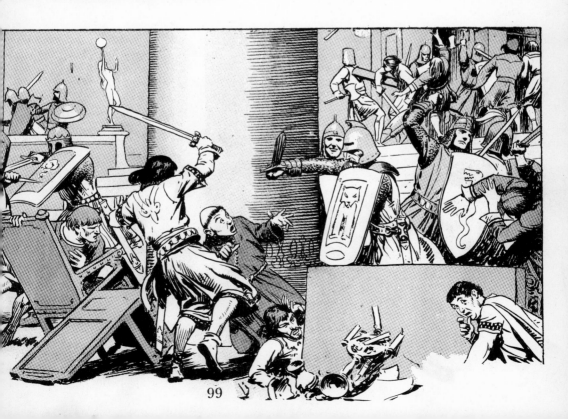

And as Piscaro's palace rang with clashing swords, it was Slith who hailed Gawain and the rest and led them to their chieftain . . . and so were good friends gladsomely met. But the battle for Pandaris had just begun, and many were the Huns slain that night.

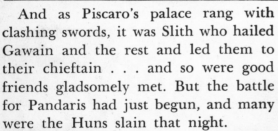

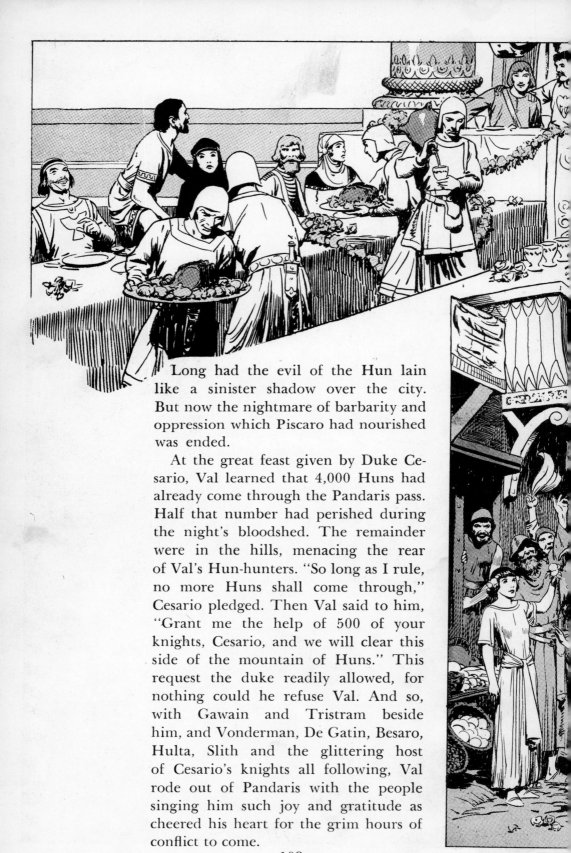

Long had the evil of the Hun lain like a sinister shadow over the city. But now the nightmare of barbarity and oppression which Piscaro had nourished was ended.

At the great feast given by Duke Cesario, Val learned that 4,000 Huns had already come through the Pandaris pass. Half that number had perished during the night's bloodshed. The remainder were in the hills, menacing the rear of Val's Hun-hunters. "So long as I rule, no more Huns shall come through," Cesario pledged. Then Val said to him, "Grant me the help of 500 of your knights, Cesario, and we will clear this side of the mountain of Huns." This request the duke readily allowed, for nothing could he refuse Val. And so, with Gawain and Tristram beside him, and Vonderman, De Gatin, Besaro, Hulta, Slith and the glittering host of Cesario's knights all following, Val rode out of Pandaris with the people singing him such joy and gratitude as cheered his heart for the grim hours of conflict to come.

102

It was not long before the troop was seen by Hun scouts. And suddenly, as the troop neared the edge of the valley, the air throbbed as the invincible Hun battle formation swept down—wings widespread in a great thundering arc. But Val had been schooled to battle in the court of King Arthur. At his command the mail-clad warriors formed the terrible wedge and charged.

Nothing human could withstand that ironclad shock. The Hun arc was sliced in two as the widening wedge drove the wings apart. And when the wedge was halfway through it columned off into two encircling jaws, snapping shut on each of the crumpled Hun wings and cutting them to pieces. Then Val sought and found the Hun chieftain . . . and the battle was over.

Val walked the night alone.

With the Huns on the Pandaris side of the pass now exterminated or dispersed into harmless groups, Cesario's knights took their leave and turned homeward, while Val and his companions continued over the high ridge to rejoin the Legion of Hun-hunters. On coming in sight of his camp Val cried out in astonishment. The valley was lined with tents. In his absence the motley army of knights errant, shepherds, peasants, bandits, despoiled nobles and impoverished warriors of all nations had grown beyond all expectation. Val's men now numbered 7,000. But his joy gave way at once to concern. Vast stores had been looted from the barbarians—yet scarcely enough to feed so many men. Indeed, Val soon learned with alarm that famine was upon them all!

Val walked the night alone, appalled by his direful responsibilities. To disband his army meant once more to open the pass to the devouring Hun and give him no hindrance to swarm again into bleeding Europe. But famine was an enemy equally deadly.

Toward dawn a sentry came running up. "Sir Valiant, the Huns are preparing to attack!" Then, in anguish at this dread news, Val beseeched: "A plan —a plan that will enable 7,000 starving Christians to defeat 20,000 Huns!" But there seemed no plan.

Hurriedly Val went with Slith and, from a rocky outpost, looked down upon the enemy's fortified camp. Within the walls the Hun warriors gave signs of unusual activity. On the far side, long supply trains were entering the open gate. "If only we could enter as easily," said Slith.

107

And suddenly Val shouted, "We can! We will! A plan! . . . Summon the council! We have a plan that can give us victory!"

The plan was daring, inspired, dangerous, but their desperate plight called

for a desperate plan. Finally Val's enthusiasm won approval from the older heads in the council. Yet even so they had their doubts.

With his head at stake should he be defeated by Prince Valiant, the Hun chieftain Karnak had proceeded with the utmost care. His base was well-manned and strongly fortified. Of supplies he had more than enough for twice his force. For weeks his fierce warriors had been disciplined in mountain combat, and incited with promises of rich booty lying within easy reach once they swept the enemy from the pass. And now the warriors clamored to be loosed on this enemy. Karnak, reviewing them with a cold eye, judged them ready.

At dawn the next day the Hun battalion issued forth, drums throbbing, spears waving and swords clashing on shields. Like a great octopus the Huns moved slowly up the wide valley, its far-flung arms reaching into every fold and hollow of the encircling hills. Prince Valiant faced his men, and words once spoken by Camoran echoed in his memory: "Soldiers, the Hun is before us. Famine marches behind. Today we feast royally on the last of our provisions . . . And tomorrow? . . . Death or plenty!"

The feast, then . . . into the night slipped a pack train led by men garbed as Huns. Next day Karnak, reaching the camp, found his enemy gone! What

he knew not was that his enemy, by a secret way, had passed him. For now, before his weakly guarded base, a "Hun" pack train was demanding entrance.

The gate opened. The pack train moved wearily inside. And suddenly the "Hun" drivers became armed knights, rushing furiously on the surprised guards as

Prince Valiant galloped in with the rest of his men . . . and Karnak's base was taken with a pack train just as Agamemnon's Greeks had taken Troy with a wooden horse! Then Val forced a captive to bear a message to Karnak. "From my fortified base, once yours. Will you dine with Prince Valiant on your provisions?" So enraged was Karnak he slashed down the messenger.

The ferocity of Karnak now knew no bounds. He had been tricked, affronted and shamed by a youthful adversary with an ill-timed flair for cheerfulness. This adversary was also cunning, shrewd and daring. How well he could fight was another matter which would soon be determined. At the moment he had advantaged himself well. He possessed a strongly built base . . . and how strongly built none knew better than Karnak himself. He possessed ample supplies . . . and this, too, none knew better than Karnak. Vowing that when Prince Valiant fell into his hands he would receive such torture as no enemy had ever before endured, Karnak then gave the necessary orders for his entire army to prepare to assault their own base.

From the sturdy Hun parapet Val's fighters watched Karnak's mounted hordes come swarming down the pass and form on the plain before the camp. Val ordered his men to their stations. "Our friend Karnak appears out of sorts. Let us give him and his warriors a lively welcome. They outnumber us only three to one. God be with us all!"

Again and again Karnak's men stormed up the earthworks only to be hacked and hewed down. And those who fell died with the curses of Karnak upon them, for with each man less his own head hung by a slenderer thread. And yet he could do no otherwise but keep driving them up. Until at length night put an end to that terrible day and the exhausted living dropped to rest beside the peaceful dead.

Morning came and a stillness like an unspoken threat hung over both armies. From the base the Hun foes could be seen gathered just beyond reach of Val's arrows, licking their wounds. It was without question that Karnak would attack again, and shortly. For he lacked the provisions to sustain a siege. To his commanders Val unfolded a new stratagem as bold as the first. It was not long after this that the gate of the base swung open and out marched the Hun-hunters, quickly forming in battle array before the walls.

In astonishment Karnak beheld his enemy standing open and exposed. He

shouted with jubilation at this act of senseless bravado. And well he might, for in open battle his Hun horsemen were without peer among the nations. Prince Valiant, young and overconfident, had committed the error that would cost him his life. It added to Karnak's pleasure to see how few his enemy were—a thin line of mounted knights. He had misjudged them to be more. Behind them ranged some foot soldiers armed with spears and sharpened stakes. These foot soldiers Karnak dismissed with contempt. His horsemen would ride them down like blades of grass. He gave a command.

A moment later both sides were charging down upon each other. It was precisely as Karnak had expected. In the fearful clash, the thin line of knights cracked. They wheeled their horses and fled in panic. Then the Huns, the fiercest warriors the world had ever known, broke their solid ranks and in a screaming mob turned at will upon the fleeing enemy. But of a sudden directly in their path appeared the contemptuous foot soldiers massed behind a gleaming wall of up-pointed spears and stakes over which no Hun horses could vault . . . and the front line of Huns fell under a hissing cloud of arrows. All was instantly wild confusion among the Huns, with the foremost lines unable to move and the lines to the rear crushing against them. Then from a hidden gully came all at once the full force of Val's mounted troops charging into the

Val's mounted troops charged into the bewildered mass.

bewildered mass . . . and the terrible, armored wedge clove like a ploughshare. What followed was brief and bloody. The invincible Hun warriors showed themselves now to be only fear-crazed barbarians, dying as all men die. Val and his men cut them down to right and to left, and pursued mercilessly those who fled. The strategy, the crash and din of battle, the struggle with a hard-fighting foe, then victory; these things were the breath of life to a warrior. But Val sickened at the terrible slaughter.

The Huns killed . . . and were themselves killed. Karnak the Ferocious was ferocious no more as he lay lifeless on the ground. Nay, the great Attila himself, the dread Scourge of God—he, too, was said to have been slain even as he marched from Rome planning new conquests; slain not by a warrior but by a woman. And as Val gazed at the field of battle, his Singing Sword still wet in his hand, he thought of green pastures and the good things in a world of peace. These were but dreams. Yet of one thing he was sure—his part was done. He had proven beyond all disputing that the invincible Hun was no longer invincible.

That night Prince Valiant had two
Hun captives brought to his tent. At
the point of his sword was a sealed message; on the ground was a casket of a
size to hold a man's head. "I grant you
your lives that you may deliver our
message and gift to your master the
Great Khan." Quickly the two mounted
and rode eastward.

And the Great Khan had no joy to
see the ghastly contents of the casket.
Nor did the contents of the message
please him more. Thus wrote Prince
Valiant: "You vowed to cut off Karnak's
head should he fail you. I have saved
you the trouble. Send more of your
generals, and all will return the same
way . . . heads for your collection.
And among them at the end will be
your own. The world knows now that
the power of the Huns is broken for
ever."

And in his heart the Great Khan
knew those words to be true.

And while the Great Khan sat in misery, Val relaxed. Calling his council together, he said: "For me this war is over."

And while the Great Khan sat in misery, Val relaxed. Calling his council together, he said: "For me this war is over. You, Besaro, hunt through the hills and exterminate all the remaining Huns. Vonderman—fortify the pass. Tristram—establish a sound and humane government for the whole region. De Gatin—divide the land generously among our warriors. Slith—let all share according to rank the booty we have taken from the Huns . . . and Gawain, my old master, just keep out of trouble."

"And you?" Gawain asked, grinning.

But Val, not answering, busied himself with lancewood and thread, colored feathers, glue, hooks, horsehair and line. His mind was elsewhere.

War is for warriors, but fishing is for kings among men—kings whose realms are sunshine, and sparkling water, and wind whispering through the pines, and the crowded silence of unhurried solitude. Thus it was with Prince Valiant. Gladly did he exchange the call to arms for the call to the clear mountain streams that abounded in this beautiful land. And with each buoyant step the cares that had been upon him dropped like faded leaves, and he remembered again that Time, the eternal enemy, had not yet vanquished him, and that it was good to be young.

And so for several days he let his feet lead him where they would—playing at wits with the crafty old trout—dining in splendor with no other company but a crackling fire and the setting sun . . . then sleeping in a bed as wide as the horizons under a roof of moon and stars.

While Val was enjoying himself in this manner, the story of his brilliant victory had reached the ears of kings and rulers beyond those who had first sent him aid. And now there came envoys and ambassadors and the commanders of armies, each bearing the same message for Prince Valiant.

They found him absent from the camp. Instead Val's council greeted them.

Then spoke one of the noble envoys. "Our royal masters have sent us to offer your absent chieftain our armies, our lives and our treasure if he will but lead us into Pannonia and once and for all time crush the Hun. Only mighty Prince Valiant can do this!"

"For behold," the noble envoy continued, "in the brilliance of his tactics Prince Valiant has shown himself worthy to be of the immortal fellowship of Alexander the Great, of Julius Caesar, of Hannibal and Pericles and Scipio Africanus! Under Prince Valiant's mighty generalship we shall march across Pannonia through a sea of Hunnish blood!"

"Pardon, sir," interrupted Sir Tristram at that moment, "but here comes our mighty chieftain now!"

All eyes turned at once, following Tristram's pointing arm. Then did the envoys and ambassadors and the others among the nobles frown wrathfully. For entering the pavilion was not a stern-faced general in glittering armor, but a disheveled, sun-bronzed lad carrying a string of fish.

"The time is ill-chosen for pranks."

"Pardon again," quoth Tristram, "but great deeds go not always with great age. This fisherman is Prince Valiant." Then was Val presented to the exalted guests and, with pride, he showed them his catch, smiling as though he considered this as great a string of conquests as those he had already gained over the Huns. And the company grew ever more puzzled.

But when at last the lad, no longer smiling, addressed the great men about him, he spoke with the confidence and inborn courtesy that go with princely breeding.

"Now, my noble sirs, I know the high purport of your mission. I know also that wars of aggression are but begetters of future wars. Here, under my hand," he said, touching a well-worn volume over which he had pored through many candle-lit hours, "is the history of the world. Here glorious victories, resplendent triumphs. Yet nowhere in all these pages can I find one single enduring conquest by force. In their turn Alexander and Caesar conquered the world. But where are their conquests now? And where those of Babylon, of Persia, of Carthage, or lordly Egypt and fierce Assyria? The fruits of conquest are but sullen enmities covering fires of hatred that smolder unseen for years until at last they burst forth in blazing fury . . . and conquests and victories, kings and conquerors become the dust and ashes of forgotten years. No, noble sirs, I have pledged my sword in the cause of justice and freedom only.

"Your nations will be secure from Hun invasions as long as this pass is held. For your own sakes give its defenders generous assistance."

Though some among the nobles were not of one mind with the young prince, all felt admiration for the courage and understanding that shone through his words. Then, solemnly, each gave oath in the name of his ruler that the pass would be defended and the Huns barred evermore from again entering and ravaging Europe.

"And now," said Prince Valiant to Sir Tristram and Sir Gawain after the noble assemblage had taken their leave, "I mean also to depart, for who knows what lies ahead either of good or of evil? To remain in one spot is to take firm root like a tree, and grow old and gnarled apart from the happenings in a restless world. So ho! for adventure!"

Then did Val bid adieu to the saddened warriors, and thereupon the three knights of King Arthur's Round Table donned their armor and mounted and rode off. And Tristram rode with bent head, dreaming ever of the fair Isolde. And Gawain the Lighthearted rode smiling, seeing frolic and merriment in all of God's things and creatures so that his eyes sparkled with boyish joy and age-old wisdom. And Prince Valiant, looking forward, sat upright and bold and shining in his youth, ready for whatsoever it willed Providence he should encounter.

And thus all three wended their way southward toward where Rome in eternal grandeur stood.

The End